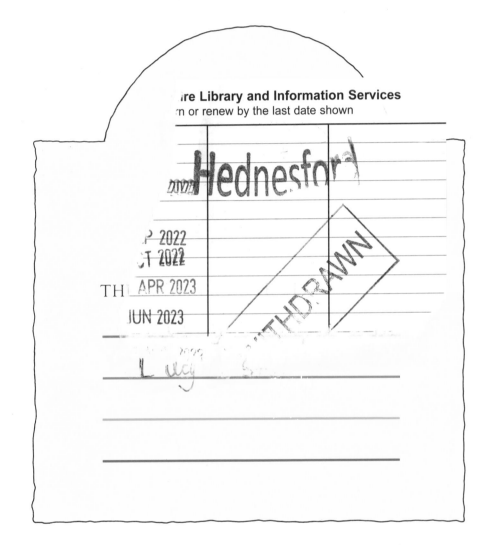

YOUR TASK

Your task is to find the treasure of Oraz by
following the right path through the jungle
of peril. Each time you choose a new path,
you will be told which page to turn to next.
But there are many dangers in the jungle.
Sometimes you can overcome them by
finding your way through a maze or by finding
something hidden in the picture. Often you
have to use your wits. All you have with
you is a rope, which you can use only once,
and your sole companion is a monkey
who is not always very helpful! Whatever
happens, you cannot turn back.
Good luck!

First published 1985 by Walker Books Ltd
87 Vauxhall Walk, London SE11 5HJ

This edition published 1988

8 10 9

Text © 1985 Patrick Burston
Illustrations © 1985 Alastair Graham

Printed in Hong Kong

British Library Cataloguing in Publication Data
A catalogue record for this book is
available from the British Library.
ISBN 0-7445-1004-X

The JUNGLE OF PERIL

BY PATRICK BURSTON

ILLUSTRATED BY ALASTAIR GRAHAM

WALKER BOOKS

AND SUBSIDIARIES

LONDON • BOSTON • SYDNEY

The dangerous jungle lies before you. But if you can find the right path through it, you will be rewarded. The Oraz signpost is no help. So go to page 7, where the path divides, and choose your way.

6

If you choose
this path turn
to page 10.

If you go towards
the mounds of earth
turn to page 8.

The mounds are the homes of killer ants! Quickly! Can you find some honey to throw to them? Then you can slip past.

Now which way?
If you take the top path
turn to page 14.
Turn to page 12 if you
think the lower path will
be quicker.

QUICK

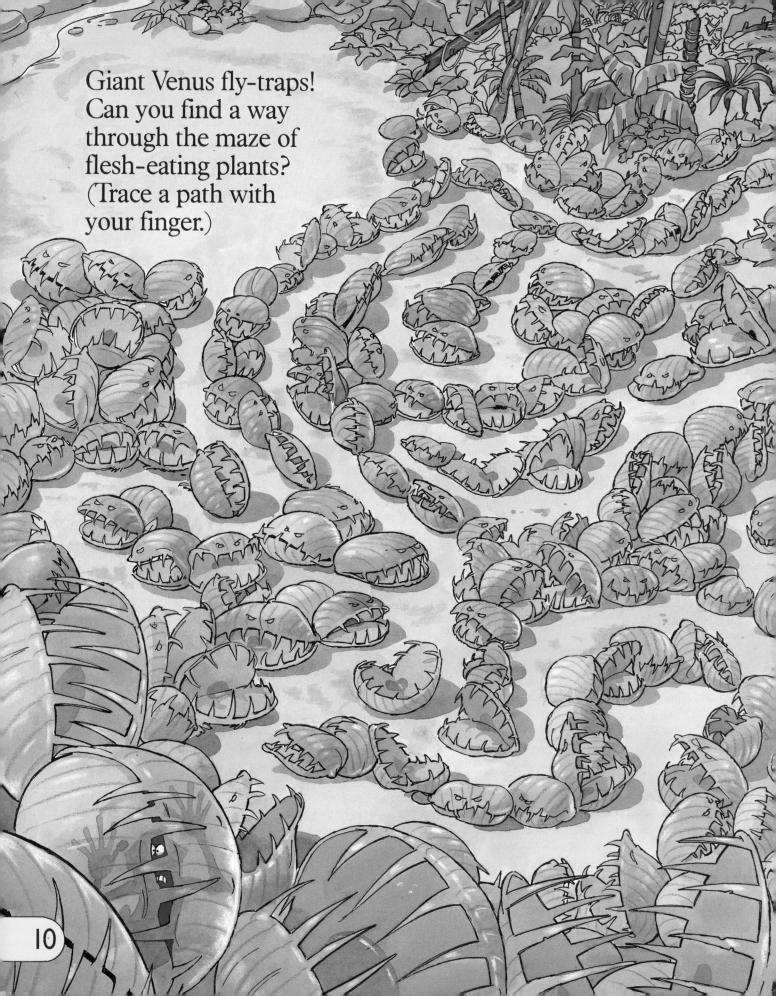

Giant Venus fly-traps!
Can you find a way
through the maze of
flesh-eating plants?
(Trace a path with
your finger.)

Take the bridge to page 16.

Take the path to page 14.

Not quicker! Quicksand!
How can you pull yourself
out? (Use something you
have brought with you.)

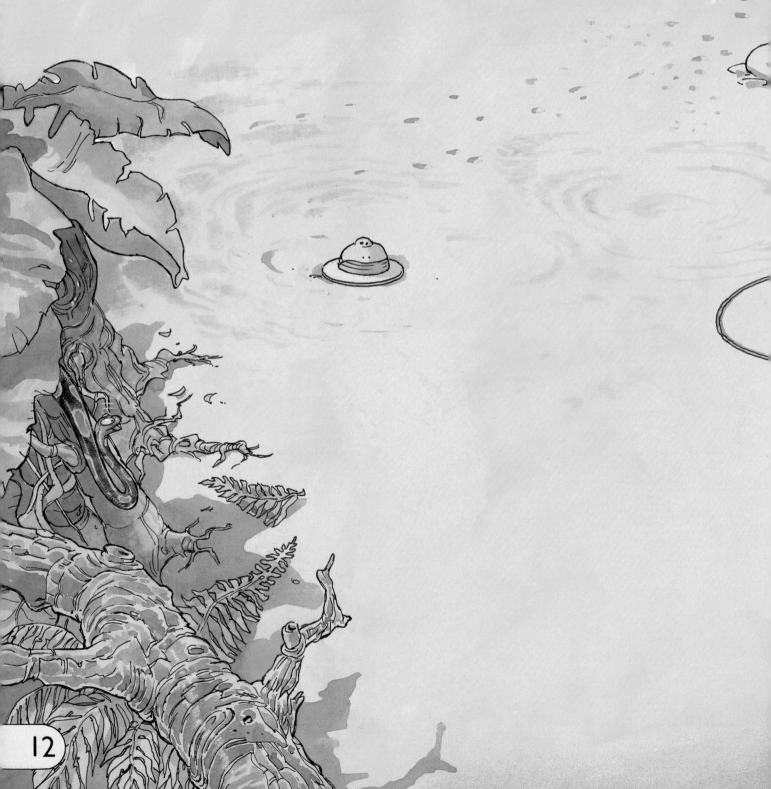

Which way now?
If you choose the
path turn to page 18.
If you take the raft turn
to page 20.

The river is full of crocodiles – and logs! Can you find a way to cross?

If you choose the path
turn to page 22.
If you take the canoe
turn to page 20.

To cross this bridge you must avoid the six planks that will break if you step on them. Find the six planks.

Turn to page 24.

Turn to page 22.

Rhinos! Find an axe to chop down the tree after the rhinos have charged by on their way to the river. Then you can go on safely.

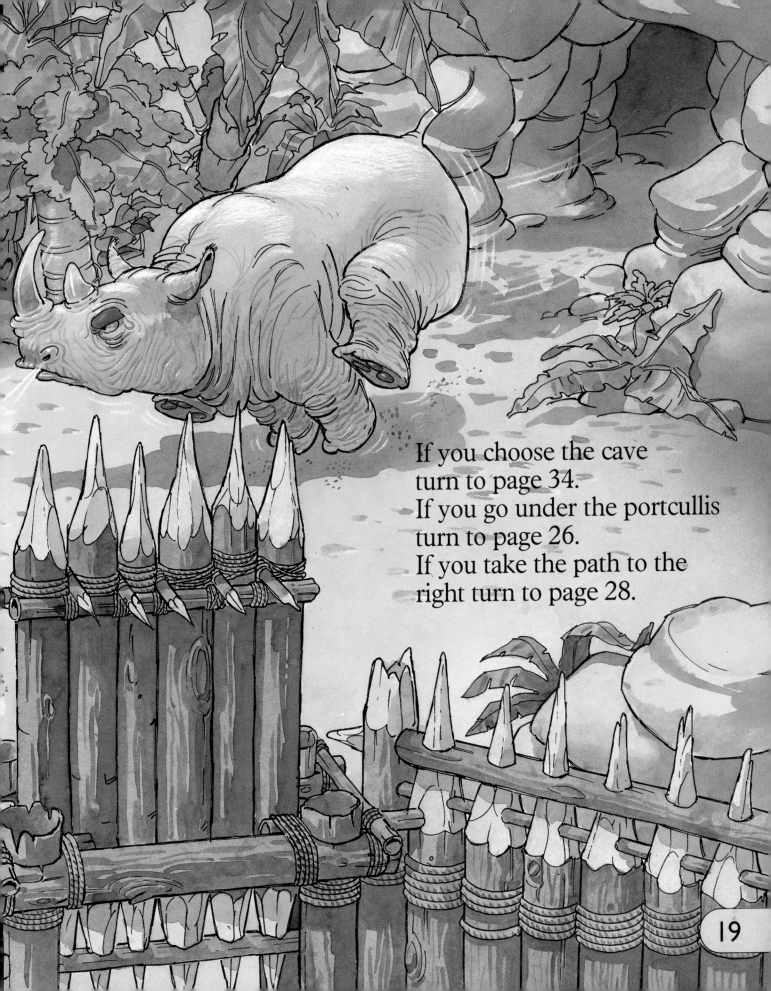

If you choose the cave
turn to page 34.
If you go under the portcullis
turn to page 26.
If you take the path to the
right turn to page 28.

You can't cross until the ten monsters stop fighting! Calm them down by finding their mates. (There are five pairs.)

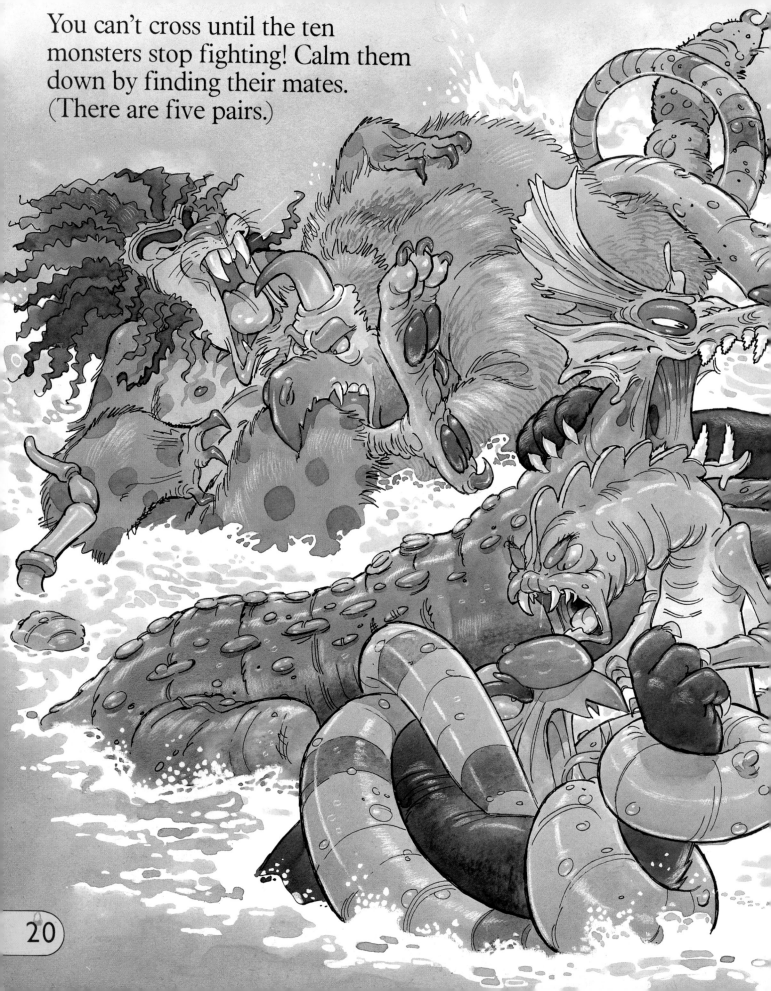

If you choose to
continue by water
turn to page 30.
If you choose
to go by land
turn to page 28.

Suddenly five pterodactyls attack! Find five spears to kill these prehistoric creatures.

Which direction?
If you choose north,
towards the glowing
light, turn to page 32.
If you go south
turn to page 30.

Look out! Avalanche! Take shelter with the monkey, if you can find him!

24

The dust has settled.
Turn to page 30 if you decide
to ride off on the elephant.
If you go towards the glowing
light turn to page 32.

Crash! The portcullis traps you in a graveyard. What can you use to dig your way out?

The archway leads
to page 36.

The path leads
to page 38.

Hissssss!! Follow one snake's body from head to tail to see which path to take next. (Trace with your finger.)

Turn to
page 38.

Turn to
page 36.

You can negotiate this huge lake only by using the stepping-stones. But beware! You must not step on the hippos!

Turn to page 40.

Turn to page 38.

Glowing volcanoes!
But there is a safe path
through the maze of
lava, if you can find it!
(Trace a path with
your finger.)

Which way now?
If you go up the path
turn to page 42.
If you go down the path
turn to page 40.

An angry lioness bars your exit from the cave. Help her find her five cubs and she will let you pass.

If you choose
this way turn
to page 44.

If you choose
this way turn
to page 42.

Dead end! This is the bandits'
hide-out. If you can find eight
bandits before they see you, you can
escape. To find the treasure, go back to
page 6 and start again!

You have discovered a fountain that makes plants grow huge. But to find the treasure of Oraz, you'll have to go back to page 6 and start again. First find a container so you can take some magic water home.

You've stumbled upon the lost land of dinosaurs! To escape, find some food to throw to Tyrannosaurus rex. To find the treasure, you'll have to go back to page 6 and start again!

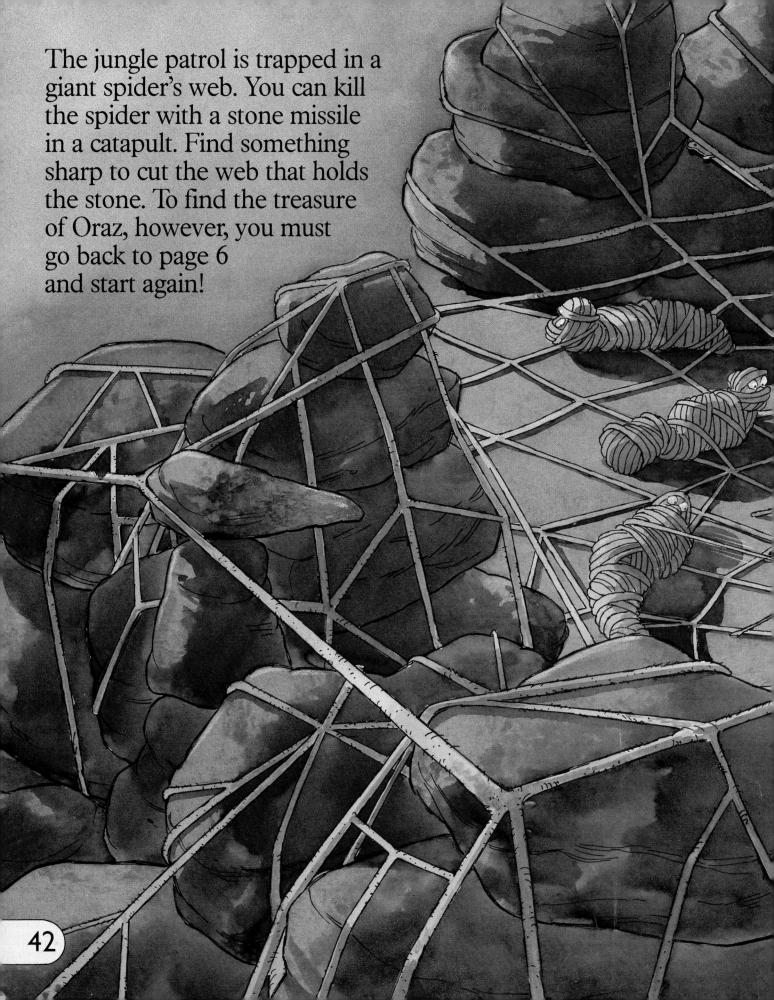

The jungle patrol is trapped in a giant spider's web. You can kill the spider with a stone missile in a catapult. Find something sharp to cut the web that holds the stone. To find the treasure of Oraz, however, you must go back to page 6 and start again!

Find
a vine
down to
the boat!

44

YOU HAVE
FOUND IT!
THE PYRAMID
THAT HOLDS
THE TREASURE
OF ORAZ!

Answers

MORE WALKER PAPERBACKS
For You to Enjoy

WHICH WAY?
by Patrick Burston / Alastair Graham

"Part adventure stories, part games – kids will be absorbed and thrilled." *Chat*

THE CASTLE OF FEAR

Your five friends are held captive by the wicked wizard and your task is to free them.
But beware! Rats, vampire bats, ghosts and ghouls of every description await you!

ISBN 0-7445-1741-9   £4.99

THE FUNFAIR OF EVIL

Mad Professor Killjoy is about to release his deadly anti-laughing gas and only
you can stop him! To find his laboratory, though, you must overcome
wild animals, mechanical monsters, death dodgems and much more!

ISBN 0-7445-1742-7   £4.99

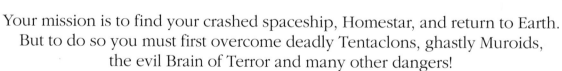

THE PLANET OF TERROR

Your mission is to find your crashed spaceship, Homestar, and return to Earth.
But to do so you must first overcome deadly Tentaclons, ghastly Muroids,
the evil Brain of Terror and many other dangers!

ISBN 0-7445-1005-8   £4.99

Walker Paperbacks are available from most booksellers, or by post from B.B.C.S., P.O. Box 941, Hull, North Humberside HU1 3YQ

24 hour telephone credit card line 01482 224626

To order, send: Title, author, ISBN number and price for each book ordered, your full name and address,
cheque or postal order payable to BBCS for the total amount and allow the following for postage and packing:
UK and BFPO: £1.00 for the first book, and 50p for each additional book to a maximum of £3.50.
Overseas and Eire: £2.00 for the first book, £1.00 for the second and 50p for each additional book.

Prices and availability are subject to change without notice.